DORRIE
and the Pin Witch

BY PATRICIA COOMBS

Lothrop, Lee & Shepard Books   New York

Library of Congress Cataloging in Publication Data
Coombs, Patricia. Dorrie and the pin witch / by
Patricia Coombs.   p.   cm. Summary: Dorrie
suspects that the evil Pin Witch is responsible for the
witches' angry behavior on the day of the Witches'
Ball. ISBN 0-688-08055-3. ISBN 0-688-08056-1
(lib. bdg.) [1. Witches—Fiction.] I. Title.
PZ7.C7813Dme 1989 [E]—dc19 88-12697 CIP AC

This is Dorrie. She is a witch. A little witch. Her hat is always on crooked and her socks never match. She lives with her mother, the Big Witch, and Cook, and her black cat, Gink.

All of Witchville was noisy and busy. Tonight was the Witches' Ball.

Cook had made cakes. The Big Witch was wrapping them while Dorrie packed them into baskets. Suddenly there was a pounding on the back door.

The door flew open. Witch Burdock and her sister Henna stood there, shrieking, "The cakes! The cakes! Hurry!"

Cook handed them the baskets. Witch Burdock looked inside. "You made them *orange*, not *yellow*!"

"Henna told me orange," said Cook.

"I never! Liar!" screeched Henna.

"Goodbye," snapped Cook, pushing them out the door.

"I wish there weren't going to *be* a ball," said
Dorrie. "It's been one crabby person after another
all week long."

"That's just party nerves," said the Big Witch.
"I'm off to get my new cape from the Pin Witch
before I do the rest of my errands."

"Don't forget me," said Dorrie. "I'm helping with
the balloons."

"Hurry! Jump on and hold tight," said the Big Witch. "The traffic is terrible."

Witches and wizards swarmed in the air. They zigged, they zagged, they bumped and tumbled and yelled. A wizard just missed them. "Out of my way, fools!"

"That was Wizard Knott," said Dorrie. "He never gets cross. He didn't even yell when Miss Malady's goat ate his marigolds. Something strange is going on."

"It isn't strange at all! Don't be a pest," said the Big Witch as they landed near the Tower. "I'll be back for you later."

The doors were open. Witches and wizards rushed to and fro with shouts and cries. Squig and Mr. Obs were mending a torn banner. They grinned and waved at Dorrie and Gink. Dorrie waved back.

"At least those two aren't crabby today, Gink," said Dorrie as they made their way over to the balloon table.

"Well! It's about time," snapped Miss Glitch. "Start with the blue ones."

"No!" yelled Plomm. "Red! Like this!" He blew and the balloon burst. Gink shot under the table.

"Nincompoop!" sneered Miss Glitch, aiming a kick at Plomm. A box of balloons spilled on the floor.

"Clumsy numskull!" yelled Plomm. He stamped his foot, just missing Gink's tail.

Dorrie picked Gink up in her arms. "Come on, we'll meet Mother at the Pin Witch's shop," she said, making her way out of the Tower. "We're staying away from *here*. This kind of crabby is catching."

The sign in front of the shop read: GRAND OPENING! THIS WEEK ONLY! FREE CAPES AND SHAWLS AND HATS!

Inside, the shop was dark. A curtain was swept back, and the Pin Witch came out. "*Who* is in my shop?"

Dorrie jumped. "It's me. I'm waiting for my mother."

"Ohhh, what a dear little thing!" crooned the Pin Witch. Her cold fingers reached out and touched Dorrie's face. Gink hissed and backed away.

"Ahh, a kitty, too! But we don't want his nasty fur all over our pretty clothes, do we? You can both wait outside." The Pin Witch disappeared behind the curtain.

Dorrie looked around for Gink. He was in the back of the shop. On a table nearby was a small cauldron with green stuff in the bottom, and a dish of pins, each with a spot of green on the tip. A few pins had fallen on the floor. As Dorrie picked one up, the Pin Witch called out, "Are you still in here, dearie?"

Dorrie dropped the pin in her pocket and picked up Gink. Quickly she slipped out of the shop.

Soon the Big Witch came out. "Can't you stay out of trouble for two minutes, Dorrie?" she yelled. "I told you to wait for me at the Tower!"

"But Mother, the..."

"Excuses, excuses! Get on this broomstick!"

The Big Witch flew home. She dumped Dorrie and Gink with a thump in the back yard, then flew off.

Dorrie opened the back door. "Are you still okay, Cook?"

"As far as I know," said Cook. "Why?"

"Mother isn't. She was, and then she wasn't. Something strange *is* going on." Dorrie told Cook about the quarrels at the Tower, and about the Pin Witch's shop.

Cook shrugged. "Well, there's nothing we can do about it."

Dorrie took the pin out of her pocket and looked at it. She got Cook's old sweater and put it on. "Let's see what happens when I put this pin in the sleeve," she said.

Cook laughed. "What a zany idea!"

"*Zany?*" snapped Dorrie. "Don't you call my ideas zany, you great overstuffed lobster!"

Cook tried to grab the sweater. "Don't touch me, you muffin-headed monster!" shouted Dorrie, running into the hall. Around and around the house they went. Lamps and books and rugs tumbled, rumpled, and slid.

Cook stopped to catch her breath. Dorrie pulled off the sweater and threw it at her. "Take your old sweater. It's too hot. It smells."

Dorrie stood still. Her scowl melted away. Cook looked at her, panting. "That's the answer," said Dorrie.

"Cook, I have to figure out how to get all those magic pins out of the new clothes," said Dorrie as they put everything back. "If people get any madder, they'll start throwing spells at each other. We can't let that happen. Will you fly me to the Ball, please?"

"Well, all right," said Cook. "But you be careful."

Through the night sky they flew. Ahead, the Town Tower glowed with light.

Inside, no one was dancing. Everyone was quarreling. One wizard stopped fighting to mop his brow, then threw his cape aside. As Dorrie watched, his scowl turned to a smile. "Gink, that's it!" she whispered. "If they get too warm, they'll get rid of the clothes!"

Staying close to the walls, they went over to the musicians. Dorrie told Mr. Obs what she needed.

Soon Mr. Obs, Squig, Viola, and the Malady
sisters began to play polkas fast and loud. The
witches and wizards began to dance, but then they
bumped, they pushed, they kicked and shoved.

"Oh, no!" Dorrie cried. "They're too cross to
dance. We have to do something else to heat them
up.... Heat! The furnace! Willi must be in the cellar.
We'll go find him."

Dorrie and Gink hurried through the doorway
that led to the cloakroom and the cellar. There in
the dim light a witch was dancing by herself and
cackling as she sang:

"Needles and pins! Needles and pins!
Crabby and cross, angry and mad—
These are the sounds that make *me* glad!
I who am my own invention
Thrive on uproar, strife, contention!
Needles and pins! Needles and pins!
This is how the Pin Witch wins!"

Dorrie and Gink sneaked past the Pin Witch and ran down the steps. Willi was asleep in his chair near the furnace.

"Willi, wake up," said Dorrie. "It's much too cold upstairs. Will you please turn the furnace up, *way* up?"

Willi yawned and nodded and turned the dial to eighty-five.

When they got back upstairs, the Pin Witch was nowhere in sight. Dorrie and Gink watched the crowd. As the room got hotter and hotter, off came the capes, the hats, the shawls. More witches and wizards stopped arguing and started dancing.

"Whew! It's working, Gink," said Dorrie.

The Big Witch had tossed her new cape over a chair. She saw Dorrie. "What are *you* doing here?" she said. "Why, how strange! I'm not cross! What..."

"The Pin Witch, Mother. She stuck magic pins in the clothes. Look! There she goes!"

The Pin Witch was dancing toward the door, singing:

> "Away, away to another town,
> Offering hat and cape and gown.
> Whenever friends are being kind,
> My magic pins will change their minds!"

The Big Witch turned to the crowd. "Now, the Witchville 'Unity in Our Community' song, please!"

They all sang. The Pin Witch threw up her hands. A shriek, a shower of pins, and she was gone.

Then everyone began to have a good time. Dorrie danced two polkas and a fandango with Mr. Obs. She was sure it was the best ball Witchville had ever had.

Dorrie and Gink flew home holding tight to the Big Witch. Cook met them at the door.

"Everything is okay again," said Dorrie. "Thank you for helping, Cook."

"Tell me all about it while I make tea," said Cook.

She took her sweater from the chair and put it on. All at once she banged the teakettle on the stove and yelled, "What do you mean, waking me up at this hour? What a nerve!"

"Mother, quick, the sweater!" shouted Dorrie.

Around and around the house they ran, up the stairs and down again. At last they cornered her in the hall. The Big Witch made a flying tackle and held Cook down while Dorrie pulled off the sweater.

They began to laugh. They laughed so hard their stomachs hurt.

Still giggling, they went off to bed.